The Time Machine Girls

ERNESTINE TITO JONES

First Edition: February 2015

The Time Machine Girls
Book One: Secrets
By Ernestine Tito Jones
Website: www.ernestinetitojones.com

Chapter One

Rrrrr----ibbet

"Guess what's in my purse," Bess grinned as she flopped herself down on the couch next to Hazel. She was chomping on a wad of gum that seemed only slightly smaller than her entire mouth. "Guess!"

Rrrrr-ibbet

"A frog," Hazel answered, rolling her

eyes.

"RRRRR-------ibbet" went Bess's purse again.

"Nope. It's a monster with green eyes and purple hair and a big snotty nose." She laughed so hard she drooled a little gum spit onto the couch.

Hazel rolled her eyes again. Bess was a walking six-year-old mess. She had wild hair, told wild stories, and thought anything that ended with a big snotty nose was the funniest joke ever. She ran a hand over her perfectly combed ponytail. They could not be any more different.

Rrrrrrr-ibbet

"Let's see if it's a monster... or Froggenstein in your purse," Hazel said.

"How'd you know?" Bess giggled, pulling

a slimy green frog from her sparkly pink purse and holding it up to Hazel's face. Hazel frowned at the germs. Thank goodness for hand sanitizer. She quickly squirted a dab into her palms and waved her hands around to dry them. "Bess, you know Grandma doesn't allow frogs or gum chewing in her living room. I'm going to have to add both of these to my list. Congratulations. I've got 25 things to tattle on you for today and it's not even noon yet."

Hazel pulled out a small notebook from the back pocket of her jeans and quickly scribbled something in it before putting it away. Her sister was going for a record today, and her mom was going to hear every last detail at dinner, as usual.

"Froggenstein and I are bored!" Bess whined. "There's nothing to do here."

She was right. There was nothing to do here.

They were stuck at their grandparents' farmhouse for the entire summer while their mother helped their grandparents pack up and move to a smaller place. And Hazel could see why her grandparents were leaving. This place was huge and old. It smelled funny, and it was boring.

"Come on. Let's play hide-n-seek." Bess begged. She pulled and twisted her gum into little pink knots.

Hazel sighed. Why did she have to be in charge of Bess anyway? Couldn't her mother and grandparents watch her while they cleaned out the old barn? Hazel knew why her mother had asked her to babysit. She was probably the most responsible eight-year-old around. Still, it wasn't fair, especially in a house with no Internet or TV. How were they going to survive?

Hazel looked outside. Rain poured down in a steady stream of gray.

"Maybe we can play something inside instead..." Hazel suggested. "I think I hear thunder."

"P----lease." Bess whined. Her big brown eyes looked even bigger in the thick glasses the doctor prescribed for her last month. "We can play hide-n-seek inside."

Hazel caught a glimpse of herself in Bess's glasses. She adjusted her ponytail so her light brown hair was perfectly pulled back.

Bess smiled at her.

"Okay," Hazel finally agreed. "But remember the rules. Absolutely no running. That means, if I find you, that's it. Be careful of Grandma's knickknacks. And whatever you do, don't hide in the attic. Remember mom said the one place we are absolutely not allowed to ever go is the attic."

"Deal!" Bess said, excitedly. Then she took off running. "Count to 100," she called out. "You're it first."

Hazel closed her eyes and counted, listening to Bess running up the stairs. "1, 2, 3, 4, 5, 6…" She smiled. This was kind of fun. Maybe her little sister wasn't so bad after all. She was actually listening and following the rules for once…

CRASH!!!!!!!!!!! BANG!!!!!!!
THUD!!!!!

"Oh no!" Hazel gasped. The noise had come from very far away, and it sounded like it came from the attic.

Chapter Two

Hazel ran up the stairs to the second floor. Then up the dark narrow stairwell that led to the attic. The old wooden steps creaked and bowed under her feet as if the planks might give way. Hazel could not believe her sister would go into the attic after she specifically told her not to. But then, why was she surprised?

Slowly, she opened the attic door and peeked inside. "Bess! You'd better not be in here! I thought I heard something break! C-c-come out... now!" Hazel's voice quivered. It was cold and dark from the rain outside. It smelled musty and damp. She didn't like the attic at all. It was spooky, and she knew she wasn't supposed to be in there.

Quickly, she turned on the light and looked around. She'd just take a quick glance to see if Bess was in there, then she'd head back downstairs before anyone could find out.

There were boxes piled on top of one another. A couple of old antique wheelchairs sat in a corner and there were mechanical parts all over the place. But Hazel couldn't see anything that looked like it had been recently knocked over or damaged.

Maybe the noise hadn't come from the attic after all.

Rrrrrr----iiibbbbet!

Froggenstein jumped across the attic floor and over to Hazel's feet. She followed its path and saw the ruffle of Bess's pink princess dress peeking out from behind an overturned bookcase off in a dark corner.

Oh no! What had her sister done? Books were scattered everywhere!

"Beatrice Samantha Smith! I see you over there!" Hazel yelled, causing her sister to pop out from her hiding spot like a sparkly pink jack-in-the-box.

"You found me!" Bess said surprised. "That was fast! Are you sure you counted to

100?"

"Bess, you're not supposed to be in here, remember? And now look what you've done!"

Hazel pointed to the toppled bookcase and tapped her foot angrily. They needed to pick all of this stuff up and fast before they got caught.

"I'm sorry," Bess said.

"You ought to be. Now help me clean this mess up." Hazel said, quickly straightening the bookshelf and picking up books.

"Th-e Arrrt off Tim..." Bess struggled to read the title of one of the books she was dusting off. She had just begun sounding words out, and she was actually pretty good at it.

"Let me see," Hazel said helpfully. "That

says The Art of Time Travel. Hmmmm. That's a weird title."

"What does it mean?" Bess asked. Hazel ignored her. All the books were weird.

The History of Finding History

So You Want to be a Time Explorer

How to Build a Time Machine in 6 Easy Steps

"Are these our grandparents' books?" Hazel wondered out loud as she put the strange books back on their shelves. She'd always heard her grandfather was crazy. Now she was sure of it. And he was grumpy too. He hadn't even said two words to her and her sister the whole time they'd been there. Did he even like kids?

Hazel thought back to a conversation she'd accidentally overheard between her mother and father one night just before the summer vacation. It was late and Hazel couldn't sleep, so she'd gone to the kitchen to get a glass of water. She stopped when she heard her parents talking.

"I just wish I didn't have to take the girls with me," her mother had said.

"Well, they can't stay here. You know I have to work," her father replied.

"I guess I'll just have to make sure they don't find anything they shouldn't find. I'm not going to relive my father's... secret. The family's already suffered enough."

Hazel wished she hadn't heard that conversation. And she wished she hadn't told her sister she'd play hide-n-seek either. Whatever the secret was that her mother was talking about should probably just stay hidden.

"Look at this!" Bess squealed. Hazel looked over. There, back behind the bookcase, was a small antique wheelchair enclosed inside a plastic dome. There were control buttons and gadgetry all around it. Bess and Hazel looked at each other. What in the world was it?

"I think it's some kind of video game," Bess said climbing into the chair and pushing a button.

"Get out!" Hazel said sternly. Didn't her sister think anything through before she did it? Hazel pulled out her tattletale notebook then thought better about it. She was going to be the one in trouble here. She was the oldest.

"Girls! Girls! Where are you?" A voice

called from downstairs.

It was their mother! Oh no! She couldn't find them in here!

Chapter Three

Hazel yanked her sister by the arm and pulled her out of the attic.

Rrrrr-ibbbbet

"I can't leave Froggenstein!" Bess said as she tried to break free from her sister's grasp.

Froggenstein hopped behind the bookcase.

"We'll get him later," Hazel replied. "Mom can't know we're in here. It's the one place we're not supposed to be."

The girls headed down the stairs. Their mother was in the kitchen making sandwiches.

"Where were you?" she asked.

"Ummm. We were just in an upstairs bedroom, playing hide n seek." Hazel replied sweetly.

"I found a video game!" Bess blurted out. Hazel shot her sister an evil look.

Their mother laughed and kissed Bess's head. "You have such a wonderful imagination! Just like your grandfather used to have."

"Yeah, she's so funny," Hazel laughed awkwardly. "How are things going in the barn?"

"You know your grandparents. They can't seem to throw anything out," their mother replied, even though neither girl really did know their grandparents or their ability to throw things out. The girls had only met them twice before, probably because they lived far away. And their mother barely talked about them.

"Are you hungry?" she asked.

The girls nodded. Their mother threw open the fridge and pulled out more meat and cheese from it, humming something quietly to herself along the way. Her thick strong arms swung wildly from her tank top as she grabbed a knife with one hand and an onion with the other and began chopping to the beat of whatever song she was humming.

"You almost blew it!" Hazel said to Bess under her breath. "That's not a video game. I think it's a time machine. But we are never going back in that attic again. Whatever it was, it was none of our business. Promise me you won't go back."

Bess nodded. Hazel wondered if she meant it.

"What kind of machine did you say it was?" Bess asked loudly, scrunching her face.

"You know..." Hazel replied whispering even lower so her mother wouldn't hear. "A time machine. I think it's a machine that can take people into the past or the future... That's what all of Grandpa's books were about."

"Whoa! A time machine! Really?" Bess yelled laughing.

Their mother fumbled her knife, looked up from the cutting board, and stopped humming.

"Huh? What did you say?" she asked.

"Oh nothing," Hazel replied. "I was just wondering if we had any pickles."

Hazel hated lying. Everyone knew she was the honest responsible child in the family, and honest responsible children didn't do that.

Their mother smiled. "You girls don't know how lucky you are, spending your summer here in the country with fresh air and wide open space, getting to know your grandparents." She handed them each a sandwich. "Your grandma makes her own pickles. Why don't you grab a jar from the pantry, Hazel?"

Hazel looked out the kitchen window as she walked to the pantry. It was still raining and she didn't feel very lucky. What good was wide-open space if you couldn't play outside? What good was playing inside if you had to tiptoe around knickknacks, grumpy grandparents, and rules? She was good at following rules, but keeping her sister on track was a different story.

She grabbed the pickles from the pantry and slogged her way back into the kitchen. Her mother was wrapping sandwiches in a bag.

"I've got to go back out to the barn," she said. "I'm just so busy. Thanks for taking care of Bess. You are such a help to me."

She kissed Hazel's forehead and opened the back door. Hazel looked around the kitchen but didn't see her sister, only an empty plate with a large wad of gum parked on the side of it. Ugh! Didn't her sister ever clean up after herself?

"Where's Bess?" Hazel asked, biting into a pickle. Sour juice sprayed the back of her throat, causing her face to pucker. Why had she said she wanted pickles, anyway? She didn't even like store-bought ones, much less these homemade things.

Her mother pulled open an umbrella and stepped out into the rain. She yelled something to Hazel as she ran.

It sounded like she said Bess had gone to find her frog. Hazel coughed on sour pickle juice. Ugh.

Chapter Four

Gone to find her frog? Her mother couldn't have said Bess had gone to find her frog because that would mean she had gone back into the attic. And Bess had clearly promised not to do that. Still, Hazel knew her sister didn't always tell the truth or follow the rules. But that didn't mean Hazel had to break the rules to pieces too.

"Just because Bess does something wrong doesn't mean I need to get into trouble with her," Hazel told herself as she calmly ate her sandwich then cleaned up both plates, flicking her sister's wad of gum into the trash then washing her hands for a full twenty seconds. "I'm not going back in there. We're not supposed to be in the attic, and I need to set a good example for my sister."

Hazel pulled the notebook from her back pocket and looked over the list of rules her mother had given her about the farmhouse. There were 137 of them, and Hazel couldn't help but wonder how many of those rules were meant to keep her and Bess from finding out the... secret. Still, rules were rules, and Bess was probably breaking each and every one of them right now.

Hazel thought about going to the barn to tell her mother. This seemed to be something that shouldn't wait until dinner. Her mother should know what was going on right now. The hide-n-seek game, the weird books... the secret. Things were getting out of control, and she needed to know all of it.

A sound like thunder clapped overhead and the lights flickered. Hazel felt the house suddenly shake under her feet, but it wasn't the normal kind of boom usually caused by a lightning storm. It was more like the slow and steady rumble of a very large engine starting, like the bulldozer hayride Hazel took at the Halloween carnival last year.

Hazel dropped her notebook and ran up the stairs. There couldn't be a bulldozer hayride in the house. The shaking was coming from the attic, all right. Just as she suspected.

She threw open the old attic door and glanced around. The ground shook violently and it was hard for Hazel to keep her balance. She looked over at the time machine. Bess sat there in her pink sparkly princess dress, smiling and waving. Froggenstein was sitting on her lap and seemed to be smiling too.

"I think I figured out how to turn it on!" Bess yelled excitedly over the sound of the engine. She gave Hazel a thumbs-up sign and motioned for her to come over.

"Get out of there right now!" Hazel

screamed, stumbling over to her sister. "We don't know how to use this thing. It's dangerous!"

Hazel yanked her sister's arm, trying to pull her from the machine. Why wasn't she budging? Bess tugged back.

"Stop being crazy, Bess! You're going to get hurt!" Hazel pulled as hard as she could, but lost her footing and fell right onto Bess's lap. Froggenstein jumped, landing first on Hazel's face then onto the control panel in front of them. A bright light flashed. It was too late. Whatever was done was done.

Everything went dark.

Chapter Five

Hazel blinked. She was lying at the end of a large field near a group of trees. The sun overhead warmed her face and burned her eyes a little. She blinked again. The sun? Wasn't it just raining? Her head pounded and she sat up to rub it.

Remembering about the time machine and her sister, she quickly stood up. Where was Bess? Where was the time machine? Where was she? Had the time machine worked?

She spotted a little wooden house off in the distance. Maybe they would know something. But even if they didn't, she couldn't just lay here all day. She had to try to find her sister. She had to figure out how to get home.

The air was thick and humid. It was hard for Hazel to breathe, much less walk. She wiped the drips of sweat from her forehead and forced her feet to move.

While following the path that led to the house, Hazel was careful to look in all directions for any sign... of the time machine, Froggenstein, or her sister.

"Hello," said a man in an odd-looking hat

who was walking over to the path from a nearby field. "Are you a playmate of George's too?"

Hazel gasped when she saw the man. It was a hot day and he seemed more than overdressed for it. He was wearing a buttoned-up long sleeved shirt and coat with shortish weird pants and long socks. Overdressed and out of fashion. Could the time machine have worked?

"H—Hello," Hazel replied nervously. "I'm looking for my sister. She's six years old, blonde messy hair, glasses..."

"Oh you mean the princess." The man said smiling.

Princess? Hazel tried not to laugh. The man couldn't have been talking about her sister. There was no way anyone could mistake that messy kid for a princess. Then Hazel remembered Bess was wearing a sparkly pink princess dress.

"Yes, yes. The princess," she replied, rolling her eyes. "Do you know where... the uh princess went?"

"Yes, she's playing with my son over yonder in the garden." The man pointed back in the direction Hazel had just come, toward a garden at the edge of the trees. "So you must be a princess then too?"

"Sure," Hazel replied, half-smiling at the idea, even though she guessed the man was teasing her. "Sir, I know this is going to seem strange, but I have to ask. Where am I, and what year is this?"

"You are right. Those are strange questions," the man answered, laughing.

"We're the Washington family, and this is one of our farms. We call it Home Farm, and the year is 1738. Why don't you know this? Did you hit your head?"

Hazel almost fainted. Either the time machine had really worked or she was dreaming. Either way, it didn't matter. Dream or not, she had to find her sister.

"Thank you, sir. I—I-- I've got to go."

The man shook his head still laughing as Hazel ran toward the garden. If this really was 1738 then they were in trouble. Big trouble. How were they going to get back? Hazel didn't even know how they got here in the first place.

And did he say this was the home of the Washingtons and that his son was named George? As in, George Washington? The first president of the United States!

Chapter Six

Approaching the garden, Hazel saw her sister with a boy around six years old. The boy was dressed just like the man she'd met along the path, only the boy's clothes were a little less faded. Was that really George Washington? He didn't look anything like the guy on the dollar bill.

Hazel ducked behind a tree and watched

them for a while. The boy was busy chopping down tall thin stick-like rods with what looked like a hatchet.

"Wow, George! You're good at that!" Bess said as she watched the boy with excitement. "What do you call these sticks again?"

"They're pea sticks," George replied. "My mother uses them to help her peas grow. Would you like a turn?"

Bess took the hatchet. George showed her how to lower it down at just the right angle to strike the side of the stick, slicing it over with one movement.

"That's awesome!" she said, handing him back the small weapon. "But I bet your hatchet couldn't chop down anything bigger than these."

"I'm sure it could!" George replied assuredly.

"Really? Even one of those?" Bess asked, pointing to one of the cherry trees that grew tall and bountifully on the outskirts of the garden.

Their trunks were definitely larger and sturdier than the pea sticks. Most stood taller than George's dad for sure, green and fruitful.

George looked at the trees then back at Bess. "I'm positive it would."

"Prove it," Bess egged him on. "I dare you to do it. The big one over there."

"But that's my father's... favorite."

Hazel couldn't believe her ears. Was her sister really daring the father of their country to chop down a cherry tree? Hazel had heard the story of George Washington and the cherry tree many times before in school. The teacher had said the story might not be true. But then, maybe it was real after all.

In the story, young George chops down his father's favorite cherry tree, and of course, his dad is pretty angry to find it dead. So he asks George about it. Even though the six-year-old knows he's going to get in trouble, he still admits to chopping the tree down because he's already an honest person. And that's what honest people do.

There was nothing in the story about a messy girl in a sparkly pink dress daring him to do it.

THWACK!

Hazel looked over. The tree was down.

"Run and hide!" Bess screamed as she took off into the woods.

The father of the country looked around then ran into the woods after her.

This was definitely not the way the story went. Was her sister changing history?

Chapter Seven

"Oh no! I've killed it. My father's favorite cherry tree!" Hazel overheard George say when she caught up to the pair. "He once told a man he wouldn't take five guineas for it!"

"Is that like a dollar?" Bess asked. "Because if it is, you're in big trouble."

"I know," the boy replied, dropping his

hatchet and pacing back and forth.

"Calm down, George," Bess reassured her friend. "I've got a plan. All you have to do is lie. I mean, come on. How are they going to know it was you?"

That was her sister's answer to everything. She was not the best person to be advising a young George Washington at this moment in time. He was supposed to be teaching her a lesson about telling the truth – she wasn't supposed to be teaching him how to lie.

Hazel tried to lean in to hear what the boy would say next but somehow lost her footing on a tree root. Quickly, she twisted her body the opposite way to try to stop herself from falling but... Smack! She landed right in front of George and Bess.

The two kids looked over, startled. Hazel's face grew red. She hadn't meant for that to happen.

"Hi," she said, nervously standing up and brushing the leaves off her pants.

"Who are you?" George asked Hazel.

"She's my sister," Bess said, introducing them.

"The sister you seem to have forgotten all about!" Hazel replied angrily. Had Bess even wondered at all where she'd been all this time?

"I saw you. You were sleeping in the field. I got bored waiting for you to wake up." Bess said, hugging her sister. "I'm glad you're awake now."

"I bet," Hazel said sarcastically, pulling free from Bess's hug. "And what about the time... uh... you know." Hazel stumbled over her thoughts and words. She didn't want to talk about the time machine in front of George Washington. He would be curious and confused. She was curious and confused.

"Are you talking about Grandpa's video game?" Bess interrupted her. "It worked! Isn't that amazing?"

"Yes," Hazel answered, putting her finger over her lips in an attempt to hush her sister. They needed to be secretive about the time machine, so she whispered, "But where is that... uh... video game? Have you seen it?" Hazel's voice was very low now, and she tried to encourage her sister to mimic her tone.

Bess pointed back toward the garden and

loudly replied. "Froggenstein and I landed right in the bushes over there. I guess because you weren't wearing a seatbelt like I was, you didn't land with us."

Of course her sister hadn't caught on to be secretive. She was born loud and had just gotten louder over the years.

"What are you talking about, princess?" George asked Bess.

"A time machine that really works!" Bess said excitedly. "It's a machine that can take you into the past or the future. You think your hatchet is amazing – wait'll you see this!"

George looked just as curious and confused as Hazel thought he would.

"Surely you're joking," he replied. "I must see it."

"Sure," Bess said, matter-of-factly leading the way.

Hazel could hardly believe her sister. Was she really going to tell the truth about the one thing she should be lying about? Hazel knew she needed to stop her sister. But how?

Chapter Eight

George and Hazel followed Bess out of the woods and back over to the garden. The strong smell of plants in full bloom blew through the air with each passing breeze. Sweat dripped from Hazel's forehead as she scanned the bushes that surrounded most of the garden. Sure enough, there was the time machine poking out from the top of one of them. How had she missed it before?

Hazel heard her sister gasp, and looked around to see what was wrong. There, kneeling in front of the fallen cherry tree, was George's dad. He stood up when he saw the children approaching.

"George," he said, motioning for the boy to come over to him. "I would like a word with you, please."

"Yes, Pa," George replied.

Bess gave the boy a hug before he left, "You gotta tell him a green monster did it with a big snotty nose!" She encouraged. "If you tell him the truth, you're dead."

George smiled. "The right thing to do is usually the hardest."

"What is that supposed to mean?" Bess asked, shrugging.

George walked over to his dad. His dad did not look happy. "George, do you know who killed this beautiful little cherry tree?"

George stood there for a moment, hatchet in hand. He seemed unsure of what to say or do. He looked at his father like the scared young child he was. Then he straightened his face into an expression of grown-up courage and determination. The girls heard him say, "I can't tell a lie, Pa; you know I can't tell a lie. I did cut it with my hatchet."

Bess rolled her eyes. "He's done for it now," she said. "I tried to warn him."

And Hazel had to agree. This was where the story had always ended in class whenever a teacher told it. And she had no idea what punishment poor little George

Washington was going to have to go through.

But the strangest thing happened next. George's dad hugged him. His dad was happy he'd told the truth. The girls stood in amazement.

"Who saw that coming?" Bess said with a puzzled look. Hazel couldn't believe it either.

Bess looked down and away from her sister. "That would never happen at our house. You can't wait to tell Mom whenever I do anything wrong, and I always get in trouble."

Hazel opened her mouth to tell her sister that she needed to stop trying to do things wrong, but instead, she closed her mouth again. Everyone made mistakes, even

George Washington.

Hazel hugged her sister. Maybe Bess hadn't learned an important lesson about telling the truth after all, but Hazel felt like she'd learned a little something about forgiving her sister. She may not be the cleanest kid, the best listener, or the most honest person in the room, but she was a great little sister, and the only one Hazel wanted.

"When we get home, I'm throwing out my tattletale notebook," Hazel said, still hugging Bess. "You are an awesome little sister, and I love you."

Bess smiled. "I love you too," she said, hugging her back.

"But that doesn't mean you can chew gum on Grandma's couch," Hazel said. "Or go into the attic, or tell lies, or..."

"I know," Bess interrupted then her mouth suddenly dropped and her eyes grew wide with fear. "Uh... I may not even get a chance. Look!"

Bess pointed to the bushes where the time machine had been hiding. George and his dad were busy tugging and prying it out.

After pulling the machine free, they both stood back and looked at it sideways.

"What in the world?" George's dad asked, scratching his head. "Now here's something you can break apart with that hatchet of yours, George. This looks like a big piece of garbage."

"What is it even made of?" George asked running his hand along the time machine's large plastic dome.

"I don't know, but do you think that new hatchet of yours can handle it?" His dad asked.

"Yes, Pa. Don't worry." George said, raising his hatchet up and over the time machine. "I'll chop it to pieces."

Bess and Hazel looked at each other in horror. *Chop it to pieces?* They couldn't let that happen, but how were they going to stop him in time?

Chapter Nine

The girls screamed just as George's hatchet came down, full swing, onto the top of the time machine. To everyone's surprise, it bounced off the plastic and didn't really do much to harm it.

"Stop, George, stop!" The girls yelled when he picked up his hatchet to try again.

George's father stopped his son from

taking any more swings when he noticed the girls running frantically toward them. "Hello ladies," he said, tipping his hat. Then he patted George on the head, "Looks like this project is going to keep you children busy for a while. Have fun."

He smiled, nodded, and walked back toward the house that sat off in the distance. Hazel sighed in relief. She couldn't believe her luck. No harm done to the time machine. No dad around to ask questions about it. Phew. Now all they had to do was figure out how to fly this thing home. But unfortunately, that was something no one had any clue how to do.

Hazel looked over at George, who was busy studying the time machine. "Princess," he finally asked Bess, "is this the machine you were talking about in the woods just a few minutes ago?"

"Yes, George," she answered. "Please don't try to chop it to pieces anymore. We need it to get home."

"I see," he said, studying the machine even harder. "How does it work? Can you show me?"

"I don't know," Bess replied, lifting the machine's domed hood and searching around the chair and control panel. "But maybe it comes with instructions."

After looking under the chair and along the floor, Bess began randomly pushing buttons on the control panel, but nothing happened. She finally looked up from the time machine and shrugged. "I give up," she said.

Hazel couldn't believe it. They couldn't give up.

"Let me look," Hazel said, pushing by her sister so she could search the time machine too.

There had to be instructions, or something, to describe how this thing worked. There was no way they were going to be able to figure it out on their own.

She looked under the wheelchair, feeling all along the bottom of the seat and on the floor, but didn't find a thing. She felt along the sides and under the control panel and that's when she spotted a compartment. It was small and partially hidden beneath the control panel, similar to the glove compartment in their mother's car. She let herself smile in relief. That's where instructions would be. She quickly popped it open, but it was empty too.

Hazel's face dropped. Bess was right; there wasn't anything there. No instructions, no books, not even a small note. The sky was growing darker, and Hazel knew it was starting to get late. They'd been there for hours and their mother was going to be worried sick if they missed dinner. Hazel's stomach growled a little at the thought, letting her know that dinnertime was already getting close.

A tear rolled down her face. She quickly wiped it away before anyone could notice. She had to be strong, but on the inside she was more than scared. What were they going to do?

But most of all, she was disappointed in

herself. Her mother had put her in charge, and she'd blown it. Maybe she wasn't as responsible as she'd always thought. She should never have allowed this to happen.

Imagining her mother searching the house for her and her sister made Hazel more motivated than ever.

She put her hands on Bess's shoulders.

"Bess, think! You're the only one who knows how to get us back. And you can do it. You got us here, didn't you?" Hazel said with the same courage and determination she saw on George's face just moments before. "Try to think back to exactly what you did while you were in the attic this afternoon. Think!"

"Hmmm," her little sister said, scrunching her face into an obvious I'm-thinking expression. "Well... I got into the wheelchair."

"Yes, good," Hazel replied in the most encouraging voice she could muster. "Go get in the chair. Maybe that will jog your memory."

Bess got in the chair and sat for a while. She scrunched her face this way and that. She put her fist up to her chin, and stared off in intense thought.

"Nothing," she finally said. She got out of the time machine and shrugged again.

Hazel groaned her impatience. "Please... could you actually think and stop pretending like you're thinking?"

"I did!" Bess yelled back.

"Well, do you remember anything? Like, did you push any control buttons?"

"Oh yes," Bess replied. "But only after I put the hatchet in the little box under the buttons."

Did she just say she put a hatchet in the little box under the buttons? What did that even mean?

Chapter Ten

Bess reached under the control panel and opened the same compartment Hazel discovered earlier when she was looking for instructions.

"Here," she said. "I put the hatchet in here."

"Good. But what hatchet are you talking about?" Hazel tried to ask calmly. Her stomach was really growling now, and she knew they had to get back soon. It wouldn't be long before their mother was going to be searching for them.

"George's hatchet, of course," Bess replied. "Only I didn't know it was George's hatchet at the time."

George swung the hatchet around proudly. "And I thank you, princess, for finding it. I thought I'd lost it this morning."

"You're welcome, George," Bess said holding her princess dress out awkwardly while doing a kind of half-curtsy.

"So... let me get this straight." Hazel said, "George's hatchet was in our grandparent's attic?"

"Yes." Bess replied. "In a trunk full of

other stuff – swords, weird helmets, jewelry..."

"What was it doing in there?" Hazel asked.

"How should I know?" Bess answered.

Hazel paced back and forth. She had no idea what all of this meant or how it could give them any clue on getting back.

"Do you remember anything else?" Hazel asked.

"All I remember is picking the hatchet out of the trunk and thinking, 'What a beautiful shiny ax this is...'"

"Why thank you, princess," George said proudly.

"It really is nice, George." Bess smiled. "I didn't think it could chop down that cherry tree, but it did. No problem."

George smiled back.

"Okay, that's enough," Hazel said, giving her sister a piercing glare. "It's a nice ax, but we really need to hurry. Do you realize Mom is going to be looking for us soon? Think!"

Bess tried to concentrate. "I was pretending I was a real princess who had to return to her castle. I got in the time machine, and put the hatchet in the box under the controls... you know, in case I needed to slay a dragon or two."

Hazel nodded encouragingly for her sister to go on.

"Then I hit this button," Bess said pointing to a green button on the control panel. "And the whole house began to shake. And... Froggenstein jumped on the button that actually sent us here. So I don't know which one that was."

Hazel frowned a little, remembering the frog germs that must still be on her face and disappointed her sister didn't at least see which button he'd jumped on. "Okay, let's try to recreate this as much as we can."

"What does that mean?" Bess asked.

"Recreating something means we're going to try to do everything the same way we did it before. Step by step."

"I hate to tell you this," Bess said pushing the green button over and over again. "But I've pushed this green button a lot since then, and it doesn't do anything anymore."

"Maybe the hatchet needs to be in the compartment again," Hazel said. "Did you ever think of that?" She turned to George,

"George, may we please borrow your hatchet? Just to see if it will help start our time machine up?"

"Of course," he replied handing it over. "If you think it will help."

"And we also need Froggenstein," Bess reminded her sister.

"Yes, of course. But where is he?" Hazel asked, wondering why she hadn't seen, or heard, that frog since they'd been there.

"He needed water, but I didn't want to lose him," Bess admitted.

"So we put him in a box down by the river. I'll go get him," George replied running off toward the river that rushed at the back of the Washington property.

"Do you think this is really going to work?" her sister asked. Hazel could tell she was getting worried.

"Don't worry," Hazel said, running her hand along Bess's tangled mess of blond hair. "It's got to work."

But the truth was, Hazel had no idea. She put the hatchet in the time machine and closed the hidden compartment just as George ran up carrying an empty wooden box, panting, "He's escaped!"

There was no sense even asking, and no time to waste. Hazel knew her sister wasn't going to leave without that frog. George was right; the right thing to do was the hardest.

Bess's brown eyes looked large and worried behind those glasses.

"We can look for five minutes, tops," Hazel said to her sister. Bess smiled, giving

Hazel a long grateful hug. Hazel turned to George. "How big is this river, George? Do you know?" she asked.

"My father says the Rappahannock River runs about 200 miles."

"Good thing we have five whole minutes!" Bess said, taking off toward the river.

Hazel felt bad for her sister. She had no concept of time. They were never going to find this frog in five minutes.

Chapter Eleven

Whoooooosh!

Hazel strained to hear the familiar ribbet of her sister's pet above the thunderous whoosh of the rushing river, but all she heard was whooshing.

"Froggenstein!" Bess called out desperately, running along the bank, but Hazel knew her sister was just being silly.

"Frogs aren't dogs," she thought, rolling her eyes. "They're not going to answer to their name."

George and Hazel decided to split up while Bess ran around like crazy, calling for her frog.

The breeze around the river was instant relief on such a hot, sticky day. And oh how Hazel wanted to just sit down and take it all in, the earthy smells, the sound of the whooshing river. She was tired. Her feet ached. Her stomach growled, but she knew she had to keep moving. She was the one in charge, and she knew if she left this up to Bess, they'd never get home.

Trying to think like a frog, Hazel ran her eyes over every tree and branch along the mud-packed sides of the river. "I doubt

Froggenstein would want to jump into the river itself," she thought as she trudged along, feet sinking into the thick soggy ground. "He's probably somewhere around the river instead."

"I'm afraid the river is too long," George said, after the five minutes were up.

Hazel knew he was right. It was time to give up. She caught up to her sister who was still frantically calling for her frog.

"Bess," Hazel said gently. "We've got to get home. If we stay here too long, it'll be dark and we might not be able to see to get back. Plus, mom is going to be very worried about us, and very mad at me for letting this happen."

Her sister's eyes filled with tears. "All you care about is yourself!" She sat in the grass and cried. "Who cares if Mom's mad at you? I'm not leaving Froggenstein. He's been my only friend this whole summer."

Hazel looked down. She knew she hadn't been much of a friend to her sister. Sure, Bess never followed the rules and always seemed to get into trouble, but she was still her sister.

Hazel remembered how excited Bess had been when she found Froggenstein inside a hollow log their second day there at their grandparents' farm. You'd have thought she'd won the lottery...

That was it! Why hadn't she thought of it sooner?

"Check the hollow logs!" She shouted to Bess and George over the sound of the rushing river. "Check the hollow logs!"

The three kids ran around searching the fallen trees that surrounded the woods at the bank of the river.

Hazel looked nervously overhead. The sky seemed darker, and she could tell sunset was approaching. They had to find that frog fast, or give up trying.

Spotting another hollow log, Hazel bent down to peek inside. There, in the dark, two eyes peeked back at her. Was it Froggenstein? She couldn't tell what animal it was, and Hazel wasn't about to stick her hand in there without knowing for sure. What if it wasn't a frog? What if it was a poisonous snake or a rabid squirrel?

"Bess! George!" she called, but they were both busy checking logs and didn't hear her. She'd have to do it herself. But it was so gross in there and she didn't even have any hand sanitizer.

Could she really do this... for her sister?

Maybe she could just tilt the log over and force the creature to come out. Ugh! She strained to pick the log up, but it was just too heavy. She knew what had to be done.

Holding her breath and closing her eyes, she quickly shoved her hand into the darkness of the log before she could talk herself out of it. The damp, cold mush smelled like rotting wood. Hazel could feel the germs oozing over her hand as she felt her way along the mucky walls of the log. She tried not to think about it. Then her finger poked into something squishy and moist.

Rrrrrr-ibbbet

Quickly, she grabbed it and brought it out. Was it Froggenstein? Only her sister would know for sure. Hazel ran toward her sister as the frog tried to wiggle its way free from her grip. Its slimy, slippery skin made it nearly impossible to hold onto, and it almost slipped free. She held it tighter against her t-shirt. Ugh. The frog germs were getting everywhere!

Chapter Twelve

"Here," Hazel said when she reached Bess. She quickly shoved the frog at her sister and wiped the germs onto a patch of grass. "Please tell me this is Froggenstein."

Bess inspected the frog, looking it over from every angle. She lifted it high into the air and looked at it from underneath. She stretched one of its little arms out and inspected its fingers. She smelled its head and put it up to her ear.

"Really?" thought Hazel, rolling her eyes. "Do you really know your frog that well?"

Then her sister gave an enthusiastic thumbs-up. "I can tell for sure because Froggenstein has a line on his head that kind of looks like the scar on Frankenstein. That's why I named him Froggenstein." She gave the frog a hug. Hazel could barely watch the frog germs being smeared all over her sister's dress. Disgusting. Then Bess gave Hazel a hug. Ugh – more frog germs. Hazel pulled away.

"Wow! I can't believe you found him!" Bess said excitedly.

Hazel smiled back even though she wasn't completely sure this frog was actually Froggenstein. She didn't have the heart to tell Bess that most frogs have lines like the one she described. In fact, frogs pretty much all looked the same as far as she was concerned.

"Thank you!" Bess said, still smiling.

"You're welcome," Hazel replied. "Now let's go!"

The children all raced back to the time machine, and Hazel and Bess climbed inside, strapping themselves in.

"Okay, hatchet in place. Check. Seatbelts on. Check. All systems go. Let's push that green button and get out of here." Hazel said, clenching her teeth, ready for the forceful shaking of the time machine's engine.

They both pushed it at once. But there

was nothing. Not even a mild rattle.

"Great." Hazel said, almost crying. She hadn't figured out this thing after all. She took the hatchet out of the compartment.

"Thanks, George, but I guess this isn't going to help."

"Sorry," he replied.

Off in the distance, the children all heard George's dad calling him to dinner.

"It's getting late. I have to go. Good luck," George said.

"Thanks for all your help," Hazel replied, sad to know it really was getting as late as she suspected. "You're going to make a great leader someday."

"Thank you. I was just thinking the same about you," George replied then ran off toward the main house.

Hazel smiled proudly. She thought about running after him. Her stomach growled. Dinner sounded good right now. And what was the point in staying here anyway? They were nowhere closer to getting home than they were an hour ago.

Suddenly, Froggenstein jumped free from Bess's grip. Hazel caught him just in time. "I think we should put him in here," she said as she closed the frog in the hidden compartment. "I don't want to have to find him again."

Bess looked down at the control panel. "I don't understand it. This green button worked fine before," she said, pushing the button again. This time, the machine shook with the roar of the engine, causing the ground and surrounding area to shake along with it.

"It's working!" Bess shouted. "It's working!"

Hazel tried to hold back her excitement. They still needed to decide what to do next. There were lots of buttons on the control panel, but which one of them would work to go home? Hazel didn't want to go anyplace else in time... but home.

Afraid of making a mistake and pushing the wrong button, Hazel tried to think it through logically. The blue button looked promising, but then what said "go home" about the color blue? That made no sense. Yellow might mean "go," but that usually meant "slow down." Red definitely meant "stop."

"What are we waiting for?" Bess shouted,

pounding random buttons all at once with the palm of her hand. "Let's go!"

Didn't her sister think anything through?

A light flashed. A loud boom. Blip. They were gone.

Chapter Thirteen

Hazel felt her head being jerked up and down and back and forth as she slowly allowed her eyes to open.

"Wake up! Wake up!" Someone seemed to be saying.

She could barely make out her sister's voice. Bess was shaking her. "Mom's calling us."

Hazel quickly forced her brain to focus. Musty, gross smell. The pitter-patter of rain overhead. She leaped from the time machine and hugged her sister.

"It worked! We're home!" She couldn't stop the tears from coming. She never thought she would be so happy to make it back to her grandparents' boring farmhouse.

"Yes, it worked" Bess said pulling her sister toward the door. "But come on. Mom's calling us."

The girls hurried out of the attic and down the stairs. The smell of hot, crispy fried chicken drifted up from the dining room. Hazel took a deep breath. There were biscuits and corn too. Their mother was sitting at the dining room table with their grandparents when the girls raced into the room. She did not look happy.

"How many times do I have to call you two before you answer me?" She asked sternly.

Her grandmother looked up at the girls from behind thick glasses, her brownish gray curls covered most of her face, but Hazel could tell she was smiling. "Looks like they figured things out all right," she said. "I told you I heard them up there." Their grandmother motioned toward a couple of empty chairs at the back of the table. "We're all starving. I'm sure you girls are too. Sit down."

"Hold on a second," their mother replied. "They need to wash up first. How did you two get so filthy playing in the house anyway? What were you doing?"

"I can't tell a lie, Ma," Bess began, "We were in a time ma--." Hazel elbowed her sister to stop her from talking.

"Ouch! Stop it!" She replied, elbowing her back.

Their grandfather looked up from his shaggy eyebrows and grunted when Bess almost said the words "time machine," shooting both girls an evil glare. Hazel jumped. She'd never seen her grandfather's eyes before.

Had he heard Bess? Was he angry? Why in the world would her sister say that anyway?

"Hmmmm," their mother said suspiciously. "You really scared me today. I haven't seen you two all afternoon, and I've been calling you to dinner for more than five minutes."

Five minutes. Hazel knew it. If they hadn't had to look for that silly frog they would've made it back before their mother had gotten worried.

"Um... Sorry," Hazel said.

"I'll never know how you got to be so filthy, but go on, wash up for dinner."

Hazel was glad to wash up. She and Bess were probably full of germs from the past and the present. Yuck. And she had gone the whole day without hand sanitizer.

After dinner, Hazel and Bess did their chores, drying and putting away the dishes that were washed on the rack. Hazel didn't mind in the least. She couldn't believe how lucky they were to make it back.

They were not supposed to be in the attic in the first place. And they certainly shouldn't have used their grandfather's time machine without asking first. Boy, were they ever lucky to have made it back on time and in one piece. No way were they ever going to press their luck like that again.

"So where are we taking the time machine tomorrow?" Bess asked Hazel as she put a wet plate into the cabinet.

"Nowhere," Hazel shot back. "And you have to dry the plates off before you put them away."

Bess scrunched her face as she pulled the plate out again. Drips fell onto the counter. "Let's try to sneak up to the attic after we finish this. I want to show you the stuff in the trunk."

Hazel shook her head. Her messy little sister was almost her complete opposite. Hazel hated germs and followed rules, and Bess... well, Bess didn't seem to mind if she did things wrong or got into trouble.

"Look, Bess, Mom put me in charge, and I've made the decision. We're not using the time machine anymore."

"But we have to..." she whined.

"I know it's boring here, but we can't," Hazel said. She wanted to tell her sister about the conversation she'd overheard, about the family secret hidden somewhere in the farmhouse, but she couldn't. That might make Bess even more curious to uncover it.

Hazel wiped another plate and put it in

the old cabinet. "We'll just have to play some other game. I promise I'll play whatever game you want tomorrow, just not time machine."

"But what about the hatchet in the attic and the trunk full of helmets and stuff?" she asked. "Do you think they're all things Grandpa stole from history using the time machine?"

Hazel hadn't thought of that. Could that be the terrible family secret?

Chapter Fourteen

The girls tiptoed into the living room and checked on their family. Grandpa was busy "reading" the newspaper, which meant he was sleeping with a newspaper in his hands. His head bobbed forward into the paper as he nodded in and out of a nap.

He didn't look like a thief. He looked like a grandpa.

Their mother was folding clothes, and their grandmother was reading a book.

"Okay," Hazel said. "I think it's safe now. Show me the trunk."

Bess smiled as she led Hazel back up the stairs. Hazel couldn't believe her sister had already talked her into going into the attic again, but she needed to see that trunk. Bess had to be wrong about the things she saw in there. Sure their grandpa was grumpy and maybe even a little crazy, but he wasn't some history thief. And she was just going to quickly prove it – and then get out.

The attic seemed especially spooky with the dark shadows of summer evening bouncing off the walls and corners. Hazel couldn't find the light switch fast enough.

"We have to make this quick," Hazel said. "Everyone is downstairs and I don't want to get caught. Where is this trunk?"

Bess pointed to an old green army trunk that sat in the corner between the bookcase and the time machine. Slowly Hazel approached it, half-afraid of what she might find inside. Flipping up the side latches, she tried to lift the lid, but it wouldn't budge. She tried again and again.

"It's locked," she finally said.

"It was unlocked this afternoon." Bess replied. "I took the hatchet out of the trunk, put it in the box under the controls then..."

"The time machine took us straight to George Washington, the owner of the hatchet," Hazel interrupted. This was getting crazy, but somehow Hazel was sure they were close to figuring out how the time machine worked, not that they were going to work it anymore.

Hazel walked over to the time machine and inspected it closer. It just seemed like random junk and parts that weren't even plugged into anything. "I bet it was because you took a piece of stolen history from the trunk and put it in the hidden compartment. That made the machine take us to the exact place and time the piece came from," Hazel said, running her fingers along the time machine's dome lid.

"I don't know. The trunk's locked so we can't check," Bess replied.

Bess looked down and away. "Do you think," she continued, "that Grandpa heard me mention the time machine at dinner and locked his trunk because he was mad?" Bess asked.

"I don't know." Hazel's voice quivered. If that were true, then it was definitely a sign they should never go in the attic again. "We need to forget about this whole thing, and you shouldn't have said anything. You've got to start thinking before you do stuff!"

"I'm sorry," Bess replied.

For a moment, Hazel saw her reflection in her sister's glasses. She hated being the responsible one all the time, but she had to. She thought about the conversation she'd overheard in the kitchen a few weeks ago. Whatever her grandfather's secret was, it obviously had something to do with this time machine. And although she wasn't sure how the family had suffered because of it, she didn't think it was right to make them all suffer even more.

"Girls! Girls! Where are you?" Their mother called from downstairs. "Your dad's on the phone!" Because their dad wasn't a teacher like their mom was, he couldn't go with them to the country for the summer. But, he called every evening after dinner.

Hazel and Bess both turned to leave, but in her hurry, Bess smashed into the bookcase and knocked a few books to the ground.

THUD!

She looked at Hazel with big, terrified eyes. Were they about to get caught?

"Go on," Hazel said to her sister. "I've got this."

Bess ran ahead while Hazel quickly

picked up the scattered books and returned them to their shelf. Such strange old books, she thought, as she straightened them, noticing that one of the books had a folded up, tattered piece of yellowed paper in it like a bookmark. It was definitely a note of some kind. Could it be a clue to the family secret?

"Girls! Girls!"

Hazel saw her sister running down the stairs. Even though she really wanted to know more about the bookmark, Hazel knew she needed to catch up to Bess. Besides, it was none of her business.

She left the note and took off down the stairs as fast as she could, first the narrow stairwell that led to the attic then down the larger one to the main floor.

"Honestly," their mother said as the two girls bounded down the stairs, practically tripping over each other to get to the phone. "You two have been acting crazy all day." She turned to Hazel. "I'm glad to see you getting along, but I'm worried you're not taking your babysitting responsibilities seriously enough."

Hazel's face dropped. Her mother was right.

"No," Bess said. "She's actually doing a great job, Mom."

Their mother smiled while the girls hugged. She handed them her cell phone.

"Hi Dad," they both said to the dark-haired man on the video-chat phone call.

"How's the country?" he asked.

"Great!" They answered at the same time,

laughing. And, for once, Hazel was pretty sure they both meant it. They were working together, getting along, and tomorrow, Hazel was going to play any game Bess wanted, except, of course, the time machine game again.

Still, Hazel couldn't help but wonder about the strange bookmark she'd just found. Maybe she could sneak back to the attic after all, just one last time.

— The End —

Hi. Thank you so much for reading my book. I hope you liked reading it as much as I liked writing it. And if you did, please consider telling your friends about it and leaving a review.

Here are the other books in the Time

Machine Girls series if you're interested:

Book One: Secrets
Book Two: Never Give Up
Book Three: Courage
Book Four: Teamwork

And if you'd like to know when new books are coming out, just have your parents sign up for my newsletter list on my website at www.ernestinetitojones.com.

Read on for more about Marie Curie.

Thanks again!
Ernestine Tito Jones

More About George Washington

The First President of the United States

The story of George Washington and the cherry tree is a very old story. It was part of one of the first biographies written about George Washington in 1800 by a man named Parson Weems. Parson Weems supposedly got the story from one of George's relatives, but Parson Weems was also known to stretch the truth a little (that means he liked to exaggerate, and maybe even make things up). So no one knows if the story is true or not.

The Time Machine Girls book tells that cherry-tree story exactly as it was written more than 200 years ago, only the original story didn't involve a time machine or a couple of girls named Bess and Hazel.

The Original Cherry Tree Story

According to Parson Weems, when George Washington was six years old, he received a hatchet as a present. After chopping down his mother's pea sticks with his new hatchet, he decided to chop down his father's favorite cherry tree too, even though he knew his father considered it special, having said he wouldn't take five guineas for it. Naturally, when his father found out, he was angry and asked George if he knew who had done such a terrible thing. George confessed, saying his famous words, "I cannot tell a lie," even though he knew he was going to get into trouble. He was already a very honest and brave person. But he didn't get into trouble. Instead, his father hugged him because he was proud his young son had been truthful about things.

A guinea – Because he was the first president of the United States, George Washington's image appears on the U.S. dollar bill and quarter coin, but at the time this story takes place, the United States wasn't its own country yet. It was a part of Great Britain, and the guinea was a British coin used for money.

Pea Sticks: Gardeners use pea sticks to support young peas in their gardens.

Home Farm: According to the *George Washington Foundation,* the Washingtons owned many farms in the Virginia area, and at the time of this story, they were living along the Rappahannock River at a farm now known as Ferry Farm in Stafford County, Virginia. The Washington family affectionately referred to it as their Home Farm.

When the American colonies declared their independence from Great Britain in 1776, George Washington led the American army in the Revolutionary War. He became the first president of the United States in 1789.

Made in the USA
Middletown, DE
01 July 2020